Once Upon a Tide

Tony Mitton

Illustrated by
Selina Young

PICTURE CORGI

Down by the seashore
Bess and I
stood on the shingle
and looked at the sky.

Bess got the hammer.
I got the saw.
We both built a boat
right there on the shore.

I got the needle.
Bess got the thread.
We stitched up a sail
from rags of red.

Bess got the biscuits.
I made the tea.
We both had a sit-down
there by the sea.

I got a compass.
Bess got a chart.
We bought them both
from Captain Bart.

We launched our boat
as the tide went out.
We both gave a wave
and Bart gave a shout.

Over the ocean
Bess and I
sailed to the place
where sea meets sky.

We whistled a shanty.
We waved to a whale.

Bess worked the rudder
and I worked the sail.

We came to the island
marked on the chart.
We searched for the sign
of Captain Bart.

We dug up a chest
so strange and old,
filled with jewels
and gleaming gold.

Pirates chased us
across the bay.
Along came the whale
and scared them away.

We followed the wind
and we rode the foam
until we spied
the shores of home.

Bess got the tools.
I found the wood.
We built us a shack
as best we could.

We made our home
on that same shore.
And we both lived there
for evermore,

singing songs
of far-off seas,
with children sitting
round our knees,

and telling stories
side by side,
'Down by the seashore
once upon a tide . . .'

ONCE UPON A TIDE
A PICTURE CORGI BOOK 978 0 552 54821 2 (from January 2007)
0 552 54821 9

First published in Great Britain by David Fickling Books
an imprint of Random House Children's Books

David Fickling Books edition published 2005
Picture Corgi edition published 2006

1 3 5 7 9 10 8 6 4 2

Picture Corgi Books are published by Random House Children's Books,
61–63 Uxbridge Road, London W5 5SA,
a division of The Random House Group Ltd,
in Australia by Random House Australia (Pty) Ltd,
20 Alfred Street, Milsons Point, Sydney, NSW 2061, Australia,
in New Zealand by Random House New Zealand Ltd,
18 Poland Road, Glenfield, Auckland 10, New Zealand,
and in South Africa by Random House (Pty) Ltd,
Isle of Houghton, Corner Boundary Road & Carse O'Gowrie,
Houghton 2198, South Africa

THE RANDOM HOUSE GROUP Limited Reg. No. 954009
www.kidsatrandomhouse.co.uk

A CIP catalogue record for this book is available from the British Library.

Printed in China